CHOCOLATE
CAKE
MICHAEL
ROSEN
KEVIN
WALDRON

BUTTER

BUTTER

D0538259

527 349 80 9

For Emma, Elsie & Emile – M.R.

For Ben – K.W.

PUFFIN BOOKS

UK | USA | Canada | Ireland | Australia | India | New Zealand | South Africa
Puffin Books is part of the Penguin Random House group of companies whose
addresses can be found at global.penguinrandomhouse.com.

Penguin
Random House
UK

First published 2017
This edition published 2018

001

Text copyright © Michael Rosen, 2017
Illustrations copyright © Kevin Waldron, 2017
A version of the poem 'Chocolate Cake' first appeared in
Quick, Let's Get Out of Here!, first published by Andre Deutsch, 1983

The moral right of the author and illustrator has been asserted

Printed in China
A CIP catalogue record for this book is available from the British Library

ISBN: 978–0–141–37920–3

All correspondence to: Puffin Books, Penguin Random House Children's
80 Strand, London WC2R 0RL

FSC
www.fsc.org

MIX
Paper from
responsible sources
FSC® C018179

When I was a boy,
I had a favourite treat.
It was when my mum made . . .

chocolate cake!

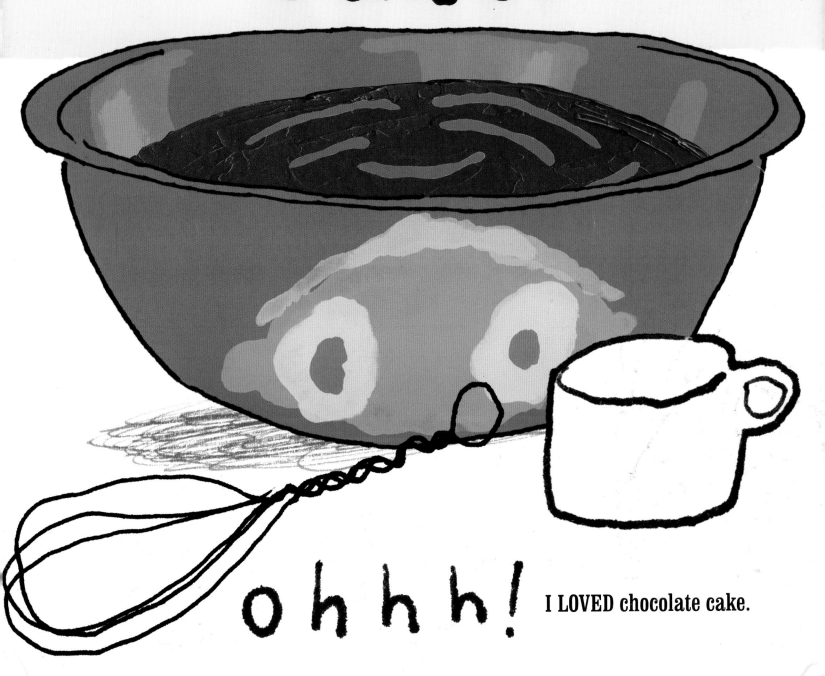

ohhh! I LOVED chocolate cake.

My mum, she says to me,
"Listen, Michael,
if there's any chocolate cake
left over at the end of the day,
you can take some to school
tomorrow to have at play time
or at lunch time."

So I used to go to school
with a piece of chocolate cake
in my little box.
And I'd be walking to school . . .

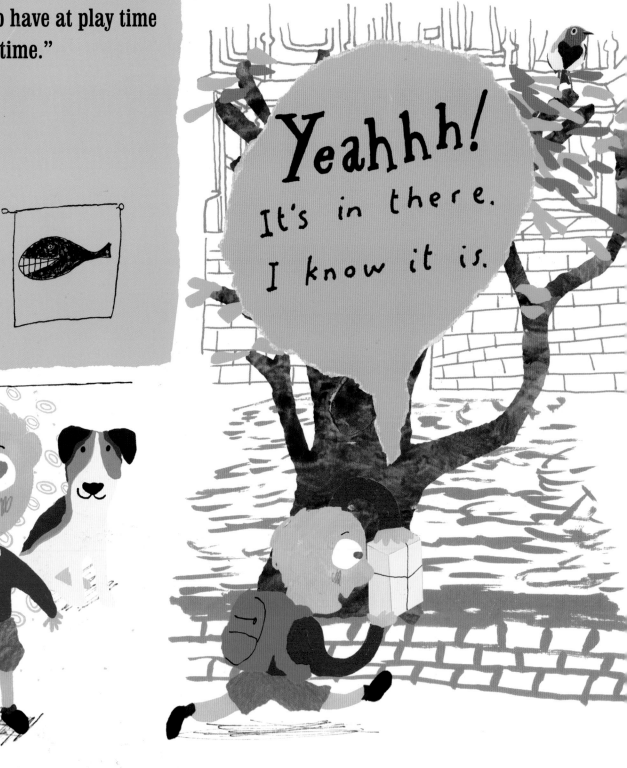

Yeahhh!
It's in there.
I know it is.

And I'd get to school,
and it would be play time or lunch time
and I'd open up the box,
take it out . . .

I LOVED my mum's chocolate cake.

And one time,
there WAS some chocolate cake
left over at the end of the day.
And I went to bed
and I was fast asleep,
and then,
in the middle of the night . . .

I woke up!

And I thought

chocolate cake!!!

Heh-heh!

Maybe I could go downstairs
and have a little look at it.

No one would know.

Are they still asleep? Yes. OK.

Along the passage . . .

down the stairs . . .

into the kitchen . . .

open the cupboard . . .

and . . .

Yeahhh!
There
it is!!!

And then I notice some little
crumbs on the plate.
So I think, if I lick the en...
of my finger, I could pick up
some of those crumbs
and no one would know
anything about it.

Chooka
chooka
chooka
chooka
chook!

Oh yeahhh!
Little sticky bit there.

Gobble! Yumm!
Mmm...
Mmmmmmm!

And then I notice
on the side of the cake
there's some little crumbly
bits just falling off.
So I think,
if I take a knife
I could just ...

Scrunch-it-all-together-
and-there's-the-crumbly-bits-
and-the-sticky-bits-
and-it's-all-gonna-go-in-there-
yeah-belly-belly-belly!

OOOmmmm-myom-yom-

OOO OMMMM!!!

Gobble!

Mmmm.

...tidy it up a little bit.
No one would notice.

SCRRRAPE!
SCRRRRAPE!

And then I notice that as I've tidied
it up a little bit over here,
then maybe I could just
even it up a bit over here.

So I take the knife again
and this time . . .
THROUGH the crispy icing
on the top . . .
THROUGH the squashy icing
in the middle.

SCRRRRAPE!

And I've got a whole slice this time –
yeahhhh!
And it's all gonna go in there.

It's a . . .
belly-belly-belly.
And it's . . .

ahhh.
A-HA-HA!
Gobble!
Mmmm. Gobble!

And now
I've got the taste of it in my mouth
and I can't stop myself,
so I go

Ya-Pshhh!
Ya-Pshhh!

And I've got these slices,
so I go

Gobble!
Gulp!

Gobble!
Gulp!

Gobble!
GULP!

Gobble!
Gulp!

Gobble!
Gulp!
Gulp!

I can't stop myself . . .

Greedy!

OH NO,
they're bound to
notice now. A whole
chocolate cake doesn't just
disappear. What am I going to do?

And don't forget to dry up.
Get the cloth.
And don't forget the knife.

And don't forget to put
them away. Plate
— in the cupboard.

And the knife —
in the drawer.

And back up to bed: shhhh!

Up the stairs . . .

Along the passage . . .
I know where the creaky floorboard is now.
So, all I've got to do is tread OVER it,
because if I tread ON it, and it makes a noise,
I am DEAD!

Are they still asleep? Yes. It's OK.
Into the bedroom . . .
into bed . . .
under the covers . . .

Aaah. Nice warm feeling:
chocolate cake in my belly,
goody, goody, goody.
And I go to sleep.

In the morning

I get up

and I go downstairs.

And I'm having my breakfast.

And Mum is busy over there

and she's busy over there . . .

And then she says,
"Oh! Michael, don't forget
your book folder."
She hands me my book folder,
and I'm busy having
my breakfast.

She's busy over there . . .

    she's busy over there.

And then she says,
"Oh! Michael!
There's something else:
there's something nice,
there's some chocolate cake
left over from yesterday
for you to take to school today."

And I went,

. . . all right.
Yeah.

CORN

Michael

And she says, "What's the matter? You usually jump at the idea of having chocolate cake."

And I went,

Yeah, it's all right... it's OK.

CORN

And she's looking at me very closely,
just here, next to my mouth.
And she says, "What's that?"

And I said, "What's what?"

"It's not . . . chocolate cake, is it?"

And I said,

D'nno!

And she went over to the cupboard.

"IT'S GONE!
THE CHOCOLATE
CAKE'S GONE!!!

You haven't eaten the WHOLE
of the rest of the chocolate cake,
have you?"

And I said,

"You **don't know?**" she said. "You **don't know?**
I don't believe a word of it . . .
Now, off you go to school . . .

. . . NO!
Before you go to school,
go upstairs to the bathroom,
and wash your
dirty,
sticky face!"

I went upstairs to the bathroom,
and I looked in the mirror.

And I saw it —
just there:

And I looked at it
and I thought, maybe,
next time we have
chocolate cake,
she'll forget about it.